Marty

BY
RACHEL NOBLE

ILLUSTRATED BY
ZOEY ABBOTT

HOLIDAY HOUSE · NEW YORK

For Evan—Thank you for believing
in Marty (and me) —R.N.

London & Marcus
and
Daisy & Oscar
and
Baby Wagner
—Z.A.

Text copyright © 2021 by Rachel Noble

Illustrations copyright © 2021 by Zoey Abbott

All Rights Reserved

HOLIDAY HOUSE is registered in the U.S. Patent and Trademark Office.

Printed and bound in March 2021 at C&C Offset, Shenzhen, China.

www.holidayhouse.com

First Edition

1 3 5 7 9 10 8 6 4 2

Library of Congress Cataloging-in-Publication Data

Names: Noble, Rachel, author. | Abbott, Zoey, illustrator.

Title: Marty / by Rachel Noble ; illustrated by Zoey Abbott.

Description: First edition. | New York : Holiday House, 2021. | Audience: Ages 3–7.

Audience: Grades K–1. | Summary: Marty is an undercover Martian and master of
disguises who lives on Earth, but when one of his costumes gives him away an
unexpected friend helps him find a place where he can be himself.

Identifiers: LCCN 2020035156 | ISBN 9780823446629 (hardcover)

Subjects: CYAC: Extraterrestrial beings—Fiction. | Toleration—Fiction.

Classification: LCC PZ7.1.N626 Mar 2021 | DDC [E]—dc23

LC record available at https://lccn.loc.gov/2020035156

ISBN: 978-0-8234-4662-9 (hardcover)

THIS is Marty.
Marty is a Martian.
He lives on Earth now.

You've never noticed him before because he is undercover . . .

Watching,

learning,

and laughing.

Marty is a master of disguises.
Look at his wardrobe of costumes!

That night, Marty couldn't find the perfect costume.
"Bad, mad, sad . . . too small!"
In fact, none of his outfits felt right anymore.

He decided it was time to be
inventive! Creative! Cutting edge!

The problem was
creativity attracts attention.

This was not a disguise.
Marty did not blend in.

This made him
STAND OUT!

"Everyone is looking at me . . .
and I kind of like it!"

But it *was* a problem.

Curiosity turned into suspicion.

Suspicion turned into investigation.

Investigation turned into . . .

Poor Marty. His cover was blown.

Hey, I'm Jake.

I'm Marty.

"You know I'm a Martian, right?"
"Yeah, I've seen you at the café."
Marty smiled. "Extra marshmallows."
"That's me! Don't worry. I think we can fix this.
Follow me," said Jake. "We need to find you
the right place so you can be . . . **YOU**."

"This is my friend Marty."

"An **ALIEN**?!"

"He prefers Martian actually, Mom."

"Oh."

"He needs a safe place," said Jake.
"I see," said Mom.

It was settled.

Marty is no longer undercover.

He's still watching,

learning,

and laughing.

This is Marty.

Marty is a Martian (and a whole lot of other things).
His home is Earth now . . .
with his friends.

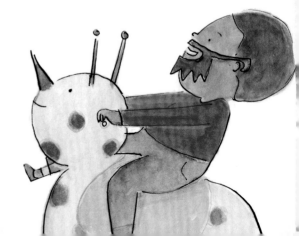